E
DE

Delaney, M. C.

The marigold Monster

THE MARIGOLD MONSTER

by M. C. Delaney · illustrated by Ned Delaney

A Unicorn Book · E. P. Dutton · New York

to my Mom and Dad
M.C.D.

to *my* Mom and Dad
N.D.

Text copyright © 1983 by M. C. Delaney
Illustrations copyright © 1983 by Thomas N. Delaney III

Library of Congress Cataloging in Publication Data
Delaney, M. C. (Michael Clark)   The marigold monster.
"A Unicorn book."
Summary: The neighborhood monster is not really very
interested in buying Audrey's marigold seeds, but he
loves her corny jokes.
[1. Monsters—Fiction.   2. Jokes—Fiction]
I. Delaney, Ned, ill.   II. Title.
PZ7.D37319Mar 1983   [E]   82-14739
ISBN 0-525-44023-2

Published in the United States by E. P. Dutton, Inc.,
2 Park Avenue, New York, N.Y. 10016

Published simultaneously in Canada by Clarke,
Irwin & Company Limited, Toronto and Vancouver

Editor: Emilie McLeod   Designer: Isabel Warren-Lynch

Printed and bound in Hong Kong
by South China Printing Co.

First Edition   10 9 8 7 6 5 4 3 2 1

Audrey loved to tell corny jokes.
She told them all the time.

She *loved* to tell them to her father, who would roll his *eyes* and groan.

She *loved* to tell them to her mother, who would wail, "Oh, Audrey, where did I go wrong?"

She *loved* to tell them to her brother, Rudolph. Rudolph would moan, "I don't know you."

"Want to hear a really good joke?" she would ask anyone she met. No one ever did.

One day Audrey saw an ad in a comic book. It said: Make Friends! Make Big Money! Sell Marigold Seeds! She wrote to the company, got the seeds, and went from door to door asking people if they wanted to buy marigold seeds. Nobody did. After knocking on every door in the neighborhood, she had sold only one packet of marigold seeds—to her mother.

Then she remembered one more house. The Monster's. Audrey found the path that led through the woods and followed it to the Monster's house. She took a deep breath and marched up to the door. She knocked.

"Who's there?" said a very low voice inside the house.

"It's Audrey. Want to buy some marigold seeds?"

Suddenly the door swung open and there was the Monster.

"I want dandelion seeds," said the Monster. "I love dandelions."

"Dandelions!" cried Audrey. "They're weeds!"

"I want dandelion seeds!" roared the Monster.

Audrey was very frightened. "Want to hear a joke?" she asked.

"Have I heard it before?" asked the Monster.

"I hope not," said Audrey.

"It better be good," said the Monster. "I eat people who tell corny jokes."

Audrey's heart pounded wildly. "If April showers bring May flowers," she said, "what do May flowers bring?"

"I give up," said the Monster.

"Pilgrims," Audrey squeaked. She closed her eyes. Her knees trembled. She gulped.

Nothing happened.

Audrey slowly opened her eyes. The Monster had lines in his forehead. He didn't get the joke.

"Pilgrims," Audrey said again.

The Monster snorted and burst into laughter. "Pilgrims!" he cried. "That's terrific!"

Audrey smiled and shook her marigold seeds. "Well, I'll be going if you don't want any marigold seeds."

"Where are you going?" growled the Monster.

"Home," said Audrey in a small voice.

"Tell me another joke," the Monster said.

"What do you get when you pour hot water down a rabbit hole?"

"Got me," said the Monster.

Audrey gulped. "Hot, cross bunnies."

"Hmm," said the Monster thoughtfully. Then he fell to the ground, laughing. "What a great joke!"

Audrey turned and ran.
The Monster raced after her.

"Tell me another joke," called the Monster, gaining on her.

"Knock knock," cried Audrey, over her shoulder.

"Who's there?" yelled the Monster.

"Gorilla," said Audrey.

"Gorilla who?"

Audrey stopped. "Gorilla me a hamburger, please. I'm hungry."

The Monster stopped. He scratched the back of his furry head. Then he roared with laughter.

Audrey whirled around and ran.

"Tell me another joke," called the Monster.

"No," said Audrey, out of breath.

"If you'll tell me another one," said the Monster, "I'll buy all your marigold seeds."

Audrey stopped. "What kind of teeth can you buy for a dollar?"

"What kind?" asked the Monster.

"Buckteeth," said Audrey.

The Monster's face lit up like a Christmas tree. He laughed and laughed.

"That'll be fourteen dollars and thirty-two cents for the marigold seeds," said Audrey.

The Monster counted his money. "Will you tell me more jokes tomorrow?"

"We'll see," said Audrey, and put the money in her pocket.

Audrey walked home thinking about how much the Monster had liked her jokes, and about all the money she had made.

"Whoever would've dreamed a monster could have such a good sense of humor?" she said to herself. "Or be such a good customer?"

She wondered what it was like to live alone in the woods.

"He must be very lonely," she decided.

By the time Audrey got home, she had thought of another funny joke. Tomorrow was just too long to wait to tell the Monster. So she got out the phone book and looked in the M's until she found Monster. She dialed his number.

"Hello, Monster?" screamed Audrey. "This is Audrey. Will you remember me in a week?"

"Sure," said the Monster. "I think so."

"Will you remember me in a day?" asked Audrey.

"Sure," said the Monster.

"Will you remember me in an hour?" asked Audrey.

"Sure," said the Monster.

"Will you remember me in a minute?" asked Audrey.

"Sure," said the Monster.

"Will you remember me in a *second*?" asked Audrey.

"Sure," said the Monster.

"Knock knock," said Audrey.

"Who's there?" asked the Monster.

"You don't remember me anymore!" hollered Audrey at the top of her lungs, and hung up.

The moment Audrey got off the phone, she started dialing the Monster again. She already knew his number by heart.